PRESENTED BY

Ann Lyons Haley
in honor of
Mr. James D. Hammett

WESTMINSTER SCHOOLS

SMYTHE GAMBRELL LIBRARY

The
Well of the Wind

The
Well of the Wind

told by Alan Garner

illustrated by Hervé Blondon

A DK INK BOOK
DK PUBLISHING, INC.

A Richard Jackson Book

DK Publishing, Inc.
95 Madison Avenue
New York, New York 10016

Visit us on the World Wide Web at http://www.dk.com

Library of Congress-in-Publication Data
Garner, Alan [date]
The Well of the wind / by Alan Garner; illustrated by
Hervé Blondon.—1st ed.
p.   cm.
Summary: Two orphaned children manage to outwit a witch
and return to their rightful home.
ISBN 0-7894-2519-X
[1. Fairy tales.] I. Blondon, Hervé, ill. II. Title.
PZ8.G226Wg 1998 [E]—dc21 97-43604 CIP AC

Book design by Jennifer Browne.
The illustrations for this book were created using pastels.
The text of this book is set in 16 point Goudy Old Style.
Printed and bound in U.S.A.

First Edition, 1998
2   4   6   8   10   9   7   5   3   1

For Stella
—A.G.

To Valerie
—H.B.

Whether far or near, I can't say, but once there was a poor man living in a kingdom by the sea.

He was out in his boat, fishing, when he saw a box made of crystal that floated on the water. He threw his net and pulled the box in.

11

He opened the lid and there were two children, a boy and a girl, with a red silk apron over them, and each had a shining star in the middle of their forehead.

The man took the children to his hut, and he washed them and fed them and put clothes on them, and reared them as his own. He cut the silk apron into two lengths and put the silk round the children's heads

to hide the stars. And then he died; and the children grew up alone.

One day, a witch came from the woods. She bit her lip and knocked at the door.

"Who is there?" said the girl.

"Where is the boy?" said the witch.

"Gone to fetch water," said the girl.

"Water?" said the witch. "Why, I know where there are springs of silver, and the water from them is a fountain that will not fail. Let the boy go to the springs of silver and, after, fetch no more."

"Where are the springs of silver?" said the girl.

"That way," said the witch, and she pointed with her lip and went back to the woods.

When the boy came home, the girl told

15

him of the springs of silver, and he said,
"Tomorrow I shall find those springs."

So in the morning he took a jug and set off
to find them.

He had not gone far when he
met a thin man in the woods,
and the thin man said, "Where
are you going?"

"To fetch water from the springs
of silver," said the boy.

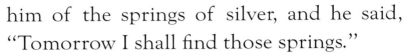
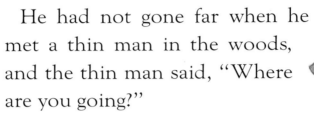

"Who hates you so much," said the thin man, "that they send you there? A great cat guards the springs of silver and kills every life it sees. Did you not know? But this is the secret of the cat: when its eyes are closed, it is awake; and when its eyes are open, it is asleep."

18

The boy went on until he came to the springs of silver. And the great cat lay there, and its eyes were closed. The boy stood still. The cat opened its eyes. And the boy went up and filled his jug with water from the springs of silver and ran home. And the boy and the girl drank and they drank that silver water; but, for all they drank, the jug stayed full. The boy poured the water onto the ground, and it rose as a fountain that would not fail.

The next day, the witch came from the woods. She bit her lip and knocked at the door.

"Who is there?" said the girl.

"Where is the boy?" said the witch.

"Gone to fetch sticks," said the girl.

"Sticks?" said the witch. "Why, I know where there is an oak with acorns of gold. Let the boy go to the acorns of gold and, after, fetch no more."

"Where are the acorns of gold?" said the girl.

"That way," said the witch, and she pointed with her lip and went back to the woods.

When the boy came home, the girl told him of the acorns of gold.

21

"Tomorrow," he said, "I shall find that oak."

So in the morning he set off to find the oak.

He had not gone far when he met a thin man in the woods. And the thin man said, "Where are you going?"

"To fetch acorns of gold," said the boy.

"Who hates you so much," said the thin man, "that they send you there? Wolves and ravens guard the oak and kill every life they

22

see. Did you not know? And even if you should kill them, there is a great worm bent about the tree; and it is a worm that never sleeps.

"Take this knife. And when you feel death near you, stab the knife in the earth and leave it."

The boy took the knife and went on till he came to the oak and to the acorns of gold.

Wolves were in the roots of the tree, ravens in the branches, and a great worm was bent about the trunk.

And the wolves saw him, and the boy felt that death was near. So he stabbed the knife in the earth and left it.

The earth turned yellow: the wolves howled. The earth turned black: the ravens croaked. The earth turned green: the worm set its teeth on its own tail and locked them there.

The earth turned red: the wolves and ravens fought, tearing themselves until they were eaten every one.

The boy went to the oak, and he climbed up by the coils of the worm, and he filled his pockets with the acorns of gold and ran home.

24

The next day, the witch came from the woods. She bit her lip and knocked at the door.

"Who is there?" said the girl.

"Where is the boy?" said the witch.

"Gone to fetch feathers," said the girl.

"Feathers?" said the witch. "Why, I know where there is a white bird of perfect feather. Let the boy fetch that and, after, fetch no more."

"Where is the white bird?" said the girl.

"At the Well of the Wind," said the witch.

"And where is the Well of the Wind?" said the girl.

"That way," said the witch, and she pointed with her lip and went back to the woods.

27

When the boy came home, the girl told him about the white bird and the Well of the Wind; and in the morning he set out to find them. By evening he had not come back.

The next day, the witch came from the woods. She bit her lip and knocked at the door.

"Who is there?" said the girl.

"Where is the boy?" said the witch.

"Gone to find the Well of the Wind," said the girl, "and not yet come back."

"Nor ever shall!" said the witch. "Gripe, griffin, hold fast!" And she laughed and went back to the woods.

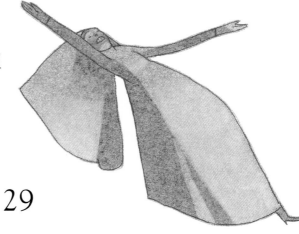

The girl set off to look for the boy, whistling. She met a thin man in the woods.

The thin man said, "Where are you going?"

The girl said, "To find the boy at the Well of the Wind."

"No one knows where that is," said the thin man. "Who hates you so much that they send you there?"

The girl went on, whistling.

She came to a gate between two trees of

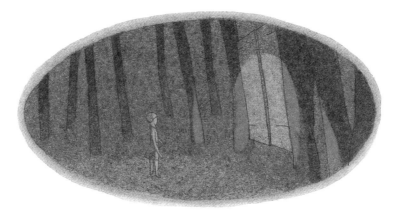

the woods. She walked about it. Then she opened the gate and walked through.

A rainbow came, so that she could not see, and when it had gone she was alone in a land of waters.

"I got from that," she said. "Perhaps I shall get from this." And she went on, whistling.

She saw a young man coming towards her over the land of waters. He carried a big mirror on his back.

"Where are you going?" he said.

"To the Well of the Wind," said the girl.

"Here is the way," said the young man, and he turned to show her the mirror. In the mirror the girl saw a round tower on an island in the land of waters. "But I cannot come with you," said the young man.

"No matter," said the girl, and she marched into the mirror. "I got from that. Perhaps I shall get from this." And she went up to the tower, whistling.

There was a door in the tower. She went through the door and found steps going down, but none up. She went down the steps and came to a well of water; but, although she called him, the boy was not there.

The girl went back up the steps. The water

followed her. There was no door, and the water rose to her ankle. There was no window, and the water rose to her chin. The girl swam about in the water, and it rose with her into the tower to a light above.

At the top of the tower, there was a white

stone gleaming, and the water rose until the girl's face was lifted against it, and she touched the stone.

A rainbow came, so that she could not see, and when it had gone, she was alone in a land of air, and there was nothing in the land on any side, around, before, behind, except a square castle spinning in the wind.

The girl said, "I got from that. Perhaps I shall get from this." And she wrung the water out of her dress.

A voice spoke from the castle. It said, "Does nobody here want to catch me? Is there nobody here who will snatch me? If nobody likes me, they should leave me alone."

"Hold still," said the girl to the castle. "You make me giddy."

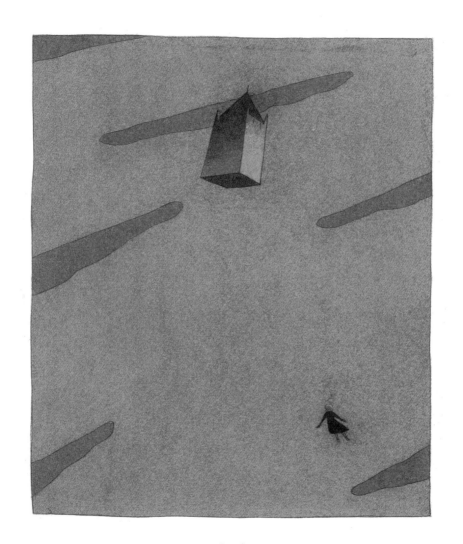

35

The castle stopped spinning, with its door towards her. She opened the door and went in.

There she found the boy; but he had been turned to stone.

On a golden perch before her, there was a white bird, and a bow and three arrows lay on a golden throne. The bird said, "Does nobody here want to catch me? Is there nobody here who will snatch me? If nobody likes me, they should leave me alone."

The girl picked up the bow and an arrow. She took aim at the bird and loosed the arrow. The bird flew to the roof, the arrow missed, and the girl turned to stone up to her knees.

The bird flew back to the perch. It said,

37

"Does nobody here want to catch me? Is there nobody here who will snatch me? If nobody likes me, they should leave me alone."

The girl aimed the second arrow and loosed it. The bird flew to the roof, the arrow missed, and the girl turned to stone from her knees to her heart.

The bird flew back to the perch. It said, "Does nobody here want to catch me? Is there nobody here who will snatch me? If nobody likes me, they should leave me alone."

The girl took the third arrow. She did not aim, but shut her eyes and cried, "Gripe, griffin, hold fast!"

She loosed the arrow and the arrow hit the

40

bird, and the bird opened its wings in a fire of flame of the witch from the woods. And when the girl looked, she saw no perch, no bow, no throne, no castle, but her own true boy and herself alive again by the sea, and a diamond where the bird had been.

"We got from that," said the girl. "Perhaps we shall get from this."

"What shall we do with the diamond?" said the boy.

The girl said, "We must take the diamond to the king."

They took the diamond to the king in his palace. The palace was all in darkness, and the king and queen were cold and sad.

The boy said, "Why is the palace in darkness, and why are you cold and sad?"

"Oh," said the king, "what are the scarves of silk around your heads?"

"Our father put them there before he died," said the girl.

"Who was your father?" said the king.

The boy said, "Our father was a man who found us in a box of crystal on the sea."

"A witch had a box of crystal," said the king. "She stole our children from us, the queen and me. And there was a silk apron about them, and on their foreheads, each, there was

43

a shining star. She went away, never seen again, and we are now in darkness, cold and sad."

"We got from that," said the girl. "And you shall get from this. Gripe, griffin, hold fast!"

And the boy and the girl untied the bands from around their heads. And the king and the queen were filled with the light of the stars for ever, and of the diamond from the Well of the Wind.

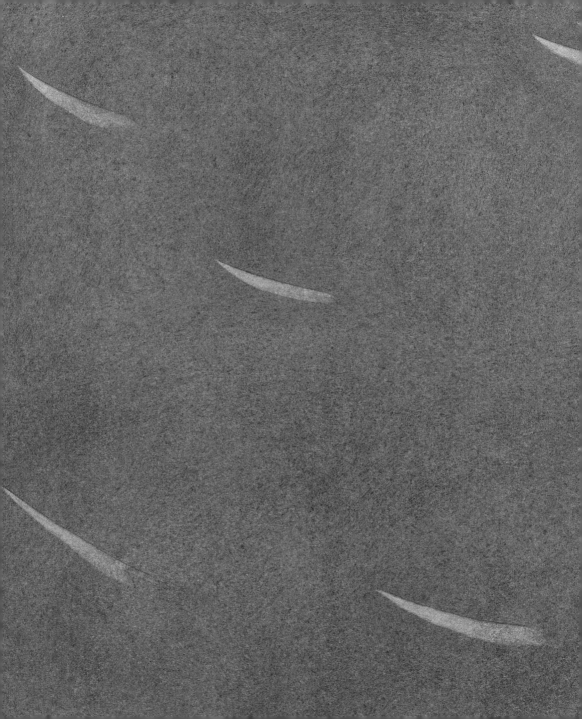